THE LAST TRAIN TO MARGARETVILLE

Paul Levinson

Connected Editions

Margaretville is a good 2 and ½ hour car ride from New York City. A train would no doubt have been a little faster, but the last train to Margaretville arrived in 1942. Now, all these years later, in the second decade of the 21st century, the only way to get in and out of Margaretville was still just by bus or car. Well, that, and walking, if you weren't going too far.

And there's also that spot in the forest.

I was not too far from it now, sitting on a hill as a soft rain made dimples on the lake below. It wasn't strong enough to do the job. I needed to swim in the lake in an all-out pouring rain before I could proceed to the forest. "To wash yourself clean," she had told me. Like that old Fleetwood Mac song, right?

Margaretville had still not fully recovered from the floods caused by the hurricane three years ago in 2011. Those raging brooks had come down from the mountains and washed many a campsite, many a house, not just clean but clean away. But not the spot in the forest, which apparently had been able to take care of itself.

I walked back slowly to the house as the sun set. I had purchased it just a year ago from a New Jersey dentist who had summered here. He in turn had purchased the house from a farmer, whose father had built the house back in the 1930s.

I learned about the spot in the forest from an old surveyor's map -- hand drawn, dated 1932, apparently made just prior to the house being built. There was a little square on the map marked "house" -- likely where a previous structure had stood, and where the current house resided. The lake was clearly marked, as were the tree lines.

And well beyond one of those lines, at very edge of the survey map, was a strange sign, an amalgam of tiny angles upon angles.

It was from a language or culture unknown to me, and just cried out for investigation. I never found out if the dentist had known about it -- he had moved with no forwarding address from his place in New Jersey. Even in this digital day and age, there was no record of him anywhere.

I showered and contemplated the lake trout I would grill for dinner. I had pulled it out of the lake just a few hours earlier. It was a lot to eat, but I was hungry. I turned my shower to ice cold -- that was the way I liked to end my showers -- stepped out, dried myself with an oversized towel, and dressed quickly in jeans and t-shirt. There was a sharp knock at the door.

She was standing outside. She had warned me, the first time we met, that she didn't believe in calling or texting. I doubted she even carried a phone. I opened the door and invited her in.

"Join me for dinner?" I asked her. There would be just enough trout to go around.

***

I got Glenn Miller's "Moonlight Serenade" on the iPhone playing in the background. Thinking about that last train in 1942 had put me in the mood for it. Glenn Miller must have been playing out of every radio in America back then.

My visitor seemed oblivious to the music. She did enjoy the trout. "They keep the lake well stocked," she said, and smacked her lips in approval.

I knew it was a waste of time to ask her who the "they" was. I knew I had never put as much as a leaf of duckweed into the lake myself. "It's supposed to be raining cats and dogs tomorrow," I said, thinking about the lake and its hard rain requirement. I refilled her glass with Pinot Grigio, as well as mine.

She nodded and sipped. "That's certainly the forecast. But there are no guarantees."

I frowned.

"You bounders are always impatient," she said. "You can travel faster than just about anyone on this planet, but you're always moaning about delays."

"I only have your word for it that I'm a bounder," I shot back, "and impatience is a universally human quality." The bounder appellation, she had told me, came from rebound, or the ability she said I possessed to make a round-trip in the blink of an eye.

"You better hope I'm right," she said. "Your plan and your safety depend upon it. But ... if you're really the illustrator you say you are," she pointed to some of my work on the walls, "then there's no doubt you have the gift. The way you capture the journey of light through the world speaks to your synchrony with the flame." She looked for an extra moment at a grouping of pen-and-ink drawings of boats, trains, and planes -- one of my specialties.

It was always nice to be appreciated. "You're quite the art critic, for just a real estate agent," was all I said. But I knew she was far more than that, and the real estate business was just a convenient cover. I regarded her. Something about her face made me feel I was looking at her for the first time, every time I looked at her. She was in her mid-30s, had long auburn hair, slightly almond eyes, and was reasonably attractive. Ordinarily, I would have thought about asking her to stay the night, or at least a few hours. Hey, I was divorced. But I had more important fish to fry. I speared the last of my tender trout with my fork.

***

I once again considered my options after she left.

I had the need, no doubt. She liked my illustrations -- this Lanterna, as she had asked me to call her -- but not everyone else in the world agreed with her. The recession had hit me hard. All five of my corporate contracts had been cancelled, and my deal with the US Mint put on hold. But my alimony for a wife and daughter she barely let me see -- that of course continued unabated. And this house wasn't exactly given to me at a discount either. I'd paid top dollar for this house by the lake, with a disadvantageous mortgage, right before my corporate cancellations began rolling in. I needed money, and no bank was likely to give a starving artist a loan.

Desperate needs breed desperate measures. I had an idea of how to get my hands on some tidy sums. The question was how to keep them, and not end up in prison for all of my efforts.

By the way, I'm not perfect, but I'm a fundamentally honest man. I would never steal from an innocent person. My plan was to recoup money owed to me by deadbeats -- three of them, to be exact, who had put my work to good use, and then neglected to pay me. They were all far wealthier than I could ever be, and lawyered to the hilt. It would take me years in court before I had a chance to present my story to a judge or jury. At least, that's what my own lawyers had told me -- both of them. I had left the first because I didn't like his advice, and the second had said exactly the same.

Good thing I had run into Lanterna by the spot in the forest. My guess is she had the place wired up in some way to give her a signal any time anyone came near it. Not that you could tell by looking at it -- just old rock, the kind they used to make those old stone walls with, and a strange glow emanating from within. It caught my eye immediately. I had asked her if she somehow had a video camera or whatever pointed at this place, and she never answered. She seemed to only say what she wanted to say, regardless of questions put to her.

I had no idea if she knew the purpose of my planned trips to New York. She never asked and I never told her. If anything she seemed encouraging, despite all of her attitude. It felt as if she wanted me to go.

Breaking into those three homes would not be a problem -- that was easy enough. My uncle had been a safecracker in his spare time, back in the day, and he taught me some things. No, the key was having an airtight alibi. Like being in the Binnekill Restaurant off Main Street in Margaretville at more or less the same time as the break-in in New York. More than a two-hour drive from here to there. No way anyone could be in those two places at almost the same time. Unless he had access to that spot in the forest with what Lanterna called the flame.

***

The sun was bright the next morning, just what I didn't want to see.

I walked the property and tried to enjoy it as best I could. The wildflowers were especially beautiful. Soon there would be orange salamanders walking delicately on the ground around the flowers. They were my favorite.

The plan for my three jaunts was to have a nice dinner at the Binnekill -- their schnitzel was delicious — talk it up with the waitresses, make a memorable impression of my patronage, and then head back to the house and that spot in the forest.

First I had to make a test run -- both to satisfy myself that this flame really worked, and to set in motion my creation of some crucial ID.

But before I could do that, I had to swim in this lake in the pouring rain, and the sun just wasn't cooperating. It continued high and shining in the sky through the day.

I walked back to the house to fetch some sketching materials. This was a pretty good second best to traveling to New York instantly. Nah, it didn't hold a candle to that, but I did so enjoy it. I started sketching a train ...

I was awoken by a big grumbling clap of thunder. I looked at my sketch. It was about half finished. I'd dozed off. I looked at the clock on the wall. It was 6:15 in the evening. The sky clapped again, like a crack on the rim of a drum, this time followed by a growing pitter-patter brush stroke of ... rain!

I looked outside. It was really coming down. I hastily stripped, ran out of the house and into the lake. The property was secluded so there was little chance of anyone seeing me, and, besides, I didn't want to risk this being just a momentary downpour and lose my opportunity in the time it took to get on a bathing suit. Rainstorms started and ended that quickly here in the mountains.

The water felt cold and good and cleansing indeed. I swam several minutes, head drenched by rain, the rest of my body under water, and then back to shore.

I dressed quickly back at the house. I left my iPhone on the table. That was the one thing that really unsettled me about this whole business -- I felt naked proceeding anywhere without my phone. This was an odd world we live in. Or maybe I was the one who was odd. I don't have qualms about swimming naked in a lake, I'm not overly perturbed about walking through a flame and arriving instantly in New York City, but I'm discomforted going anywhere without my phone. But I didn't have a choice in this case.

The last thing I needed was some NSA or whatever data tracking organization having evidence from the GPS in my phone that I had been in two places at almost the same time. I did take the big wad of cash I had put aside for this occasion, and some non-digital old-fashioned IDs from my wallet.

I proceeded to the spot in the forest.

***

It was a 15-minute careful walk through a dense forest, mostly of pine and maple, and an intense underbrush that could trip you up if you weren't careful. It was highly unlikely that anyone would stumble on the spot -- I of course had arrived here the first time guided by the surveyor's map.

The sun was a few minutes from setting when I reached the spot. The glow from the inside of the structure was soft and gently flickering, the kind of light a bulb on the ceiling might make if there was a fan slowly spinning below it. But this light came from a flame in an old stone fireplace on the ground -- a single, wide flame about 10 feet high.

I knew about the heat. I had been here before. Lanterna had assured me that once I got closer to it, about to walk into it, all would be cool -- and then I would be transported. Up until now, I had been glad that Lanterna had told me she would not be here, because I didn't need her that much into my business. But now I suddenly felt otherwise. I breathed in deeply. This was not a time to panic. If I proceeded into the flame and felt at all singed, I could quickly withdraw. I wouldn't just stand there like a bride in some traditions and allow myself to get burned to death by the flame.

I walked to the flame. I felt the heat and involuntarily shut my eyes, but then I opened them and squinted. I wanted to see what was happening. And it suddenly felt cool. I opened my eyes wide and saw colors changing to shades of every possible tomato -- red, orange, yellow, everything in between. I took one step further and found myself in what looked and smelled like a dank basement.

***

I gave my eyes and myself a few seconds to adjust to the new surroundings. I was in a dimly lit room of some sort, no longer in the forest. But was it the tunnel under Fordham University in the Bronx?

Lanterna had given me a paper map, which I had memorized and carried in my pocket for back-up. I had grown up in the neighbourhood, on the other side of White Plains Road. I had also extensively researched the place, and all of this coincided with what I had seen of Fordham the few times I had guest-lectured in art classes over the years. Keating Hall was constructed in the 1930s on Fordham University's Rose Hill campus in the Bronx -- about 30 minutes by train from the first home I intended to burglarize, in Yonkers. I wouldn't have minded a closer point of entry, but beggars -- or bounders, to use Lanterna's term -- couldn't be choosers.

Tunnels beneath Keating definitely existed. I looked at the multi-hued shimmering flame that was now a few steps behind me. The question was where exactly were it and I in the Keating tunnel system -- assuming I indeed was now in the tunnels under Keating.

I hoped I was not too far from the University Bookstore above as indicated on the map. It called for me to walk about 15 feet, open a door, climb a staircase, walk several hundred feet, climb another set of stairs, open a door and that would bring me to a lower level of Keating which snaked and turned and eventually brought me near WFUV, Fordham's radio station.

Good thing I had brought my powerful little LED flashlight

with me -- I had almost left it in Margaretville, because I was so accustomed to using the flashlight app on my phone, which I had left at home. I didn't see light in the tunnels until I reached the level with the radio station. And I didn't know I was at Fordham University for sure until I saw the FUV offices. I sauntered by, so as not to attract attention, but I had all I could do not to jump in the air and shout "Yes!!" This insane flame thing had actually worked for me!

The University Bookstore was right across the street from Keating Hall. I had checked on its hours -- it was open until 9pm on this summer evening, because summer school was still in session. I walked into the bookstore -- it was empty of customers, not a good thing -- but I quickly saw what I needed. I picked up the cheapest camera with Internet connections, brought it to the cashier -- a redhead with freckles and white pants that looked like they'd been spray painted on -- and made my purchase. I slipped in the batteries, made sure the camera and its Internet connection worked, and walked a suitable distance away from the counter.

Now came the hard part. I had to wait for some guy, any guy, to make a purchase, and hope that he displayed a university ID card to get a student or faculty discount. But how long could I wait without looking suspicious? I walked a few steps further away from the counter and pretended to carefully read the start-up instructions on my camera, though I knew exactly how it worked.

Some five minutes later, a guy in his twenties, likely a student, entered the bookstore. He picked up a gym bag -- they were on sale -- and approached the counter. He pulled out his wallet and paid with cash. Great, no help at all.

I ambled even further away and pretended to be engrossed in some books required for a chem class. Three more customers came in, and not a single one showed a university ID card. I'd been here more than 15 minutes already. I had to wait as long as was necessary.

Fortunately, the redhead seemed oblivious to me, devoting every ounce of her attention when she wasn't ringing up a sale to her smartphone and some messaging that was making her smile, frown, and pout in slow procession.

A man entered the bookstore. I walked a little closer to the cashier so I could get a picture if an ID card was displayed. The man noticed me, and gestured that I should go first. I smiled graciously and muttered "after you." He proceeded to the cashier, picked up an oversized sweatshirt that was on sale, and gave it to the cashier.

"Do you have a Fordham ID?" she asked, sweetly.

"Absolutely," the man replied, and produced his ID.

Yes!

"Thank you, Professor Pilant," the redhead said, "this gives you a 25% discount." She gave the ID back to him.

And I left the bookstore. I had what I needed. Four photos of the professor's ID, which I looked at in the cool moonlight on the street outside of the bookstore. I uploaded the photos to Google Drive, Dropbox, and two other sites, just to be sure. I walked to Keating, and dropped the camera in a trash receptacle. When I got back to Margaretville, I'd access those photos, doctor them up, and use them to make a Fordham faculty ID for myself. Next time I traveled back here, I'd be able to leave the campus, pay a visit to the deadbeat's house in Yonkers, and come right back to this campus with no security guard questioning what I was doing here after I displayed my new ID.

∗∗∗

The trip back to the house in Margaretville was a piece of cake. So was accessing the photos I had uploaded at Fordham, and then producing a Fordham ID with my photo and Pilant's name. I also produced an ID with my photo and my name, and my photo and a bogus name. Depending on who asked to see it, I'd make a decision about which one to present. With any luck, the security guard would not know what Professor Pilant looked like. Fordham University was a big school.

I was ready to go the next morning. Unfortunately the weather was not. I suffered through six sunny days. I was like a damn farmer already, praying for rain. I cursed and railed against the good weather, and tried to console myself with the thought that even miracles come with strings attached.

I consoled myself further with the greatest continuing consolation in my life, my drawings. I finished the last train to Margaretville -- that's what that drawing had become -- and began to sketch something else. Then I put that aside and started a watercolor. It was something I'd never attempted before -- the soft, blurry shades of a dozen tomatoes, each a slightly different color--

And I looked outside and saw it was beginning to rain. I almost hated to be pulled away from my painting, but the rain took precedence. I took off my clothes and waded into the lake. It was raining hard now.

The bathing would be good for me to go through the flame for 24 hours, Lanterna had told me. It was now about 3 in the afternoon. My next stop would be the Binnekill Restaurant for dinner at 6pm.

***

Jaeger schnitzel -- hunter's schnitzel, not breaded, just veal in a mushroom sauce -- has long been one of my favorite dishes. I'd ordered it the two previous times I'd been in the Binnekill in the past year, and it had been mouth-watering both times.

"Good to see you again," the hostess who was also a waitress greeted me with a smile, "haven't seen you here in a while." She was blonde, long neck, long hair, in her early 30s, and I thought what I always think when I see a woman like that. I'd like to paint her in the nude -- tell her I was using her as a model for a Greek goddess -- and go on to do more. But tonight I had even more pressing matters on the table.

"Yeah, I've been busy with my illustrations," I said, and ordered the Jaeger schnitzel.

"Are you an artist? I didn't know that," she said, and smiled at me again.

So far, this was going exactly as if my goal were indeed to paint and bed her.

"What kind of things do you paint?" she asked me.

"Nature, in all its forms," I replied. "And I also have an eye for transportation technology." At this point, I sometimes threw in a joke about having an affinity for cabooses, but I refrained this time.

"You have a good place for the nature up here," she said. "Is your work on display anywhere?"

"Just in a few galleries here and there," I said. "I'm building up my catalogue."

She nodded and left to place my order. She returned with it about 10 minutes later.

"Jaeger schnitzel," she said, and placed the dish on my table with a flourish. "Can I get you anything else? A little beer with your schnitzel?"

If only I didn't have plans for this evening. But I had only my fantasies that she would be willing to pose for me, and it likely wouldn't have happened this evening in any case.

"No, I'm fine," I replied. I needed a clear head for the rest of the evening. I figured this conversation would be more than enough for her to remember me if anyone thought I was in New York just minutes from now.

"You know, my husband is an art dealer," she said.

"Really? You're kidding!"

"No, it's true," she said. "And I'd be happy to tell him about your work. Do you have a card?"

"I certainly do," I said and reached into my pocket. We exchanged cards. Funny how this world works -- just when I was about to steal someone's money to pay my bills, a possible source of income pops up unexpectedly at a restaurant. But whatever her husband could do for me, it would likely provide a pittance of the money in hand I would be getting in New York tonight before the end of the hour.

I finished my schnitzel quickly, declined dessert, and left a 50% tip. She would 100% remember me.

***

The walk to the spot in the forest was no problem, as was the walk through the tunnels of Keating and my exit from the campus. No one asked for my ID -- no one cares who are you when you're leaving.

I caught the Metro North at the Fordham Road station and took it down to 125th Street. I switched to the uptown Harlem line to Ludlow. I had all of this timed to under 30 minutes. A cab would have been a little faster, but I didn't need a cabbie complicating matters as a witness to my being here.

I exited the station and walked uphill to the deadbeat's house. I had picked this guy first because his house would be the easiest. It was in Yonkers, the closest to Fordham. I knew where he kept his stash of cash -- in a drawer in his bedroom, which I had seen through an open door the one time I had previously been in the house and he paid me. And I knew the layout of the house outside and the rock under which he kept his extra key.

I had been hired to thoroughly sketch the house when the deadbeat thought he was putting it up for sale, and had come upon the key when I had moved a few rocks to getter a better vantage point for one of the sketches. And I also knew that he and his family were currently in Maine in a summer house.

Still, I had to be very careful. The last thing I needed was a nosy neighbour calling the cops. They wouldn't be impressed at all with my Fordham ID.

Fortunately, the house was unattached. I walked around to the side which had the rock. I had to do this quickly. Every minute that I stayed here increased the possibility of someone noticing there was someone in the house.

The key was in a plastic bag where it should have been. I took it out, walked to the side entrance, and unlocked the door. No alarms that I could hear went off. I was in!

I walked to the bedroom, opened the drawer, and helped myself to the hundred dollar bills in several envelopes. I took as many envelopes as the deep pockets in my pants and jacket could carry. I figured I had seven or eight thousand dollars here. That should help pay some bills. It certainly covered the money the deadbeat owed me, and a little more for my troubles.

I walked quickly back to the door, and spotted another bunch of envelopes in an open drawer. I had room for a few more. I took one of the envelopes. It didn't feel like it had money. It was filled with medical bills--

A car drove by -- I could see the lights outside. I froze.

Fortunately the car kept moving. I resumed breathing.

I read through the medical bills quickly. The deadbeat's boy had a serious heart condition that required repeated surgery. Repeated surgery that was very expensive. Didn't this guy's family qualify under Obamacare? I couldn't tell. The deadbeat was a self-employed contractor. He clearly cut corners with everything, and apparently not only with the money he owed me but in getting decent health insurance. The heart surgeries for his son were draining him dry.

His boy needed heart surgery. But my heart, though often muddled, was I guess in the right place when it came to this deadbeat. I couldn't take thousands of dollars of his money and leave his son to the wolves of uncertain medical care. I cursed loudly, was glad there was no nearby neighbour to hear it, and returned the envelopes with the money to the bedroom drawer.

I left the house and walked quickly down to the Ludlow station to take the trains back to Fordham. Of all the rotten luck -- but I'd just have to do better with the next deadbeat. I briefly considered whether I should continue on the train to Grand Central, and pay a visit to the second deadbeat's place, which was in a ritzy highrise in lower Manhattan. Tempting-- but no, I needed to vet that plan. It was dangerous just tacking it on to what I was doing tonight.

I was back outside the Fordham campus 26 minutes later.

***

I approached the security guard and casually waved my ID -- the one with my picture and Pilant's name. The guard didn't even look at it. I could have had a picture of George Washington on the card.

***

The flame in the tunnel way under Keating Hall looked especially beautiful tonight. I'd never seen such a spectrum of light. And so did the flame in the forest in Margaretville -- a mirror image of the Keating Hall beauty, which made it just as beautiful itself.

I ran into a string of sunny days. Even the wildflowers looked parched.

I busied myself with my watercolors. I had several of them now. My phone rang one day in the late afternoon. The number looked slightly familiar. It was the husband of the blonde in the Binnekill. He wanted to look at my work, and was wondering if he could come right over. "Sure," I told him, and gave him directions.

He pulled up in a Mini Cooper about 15 minutes later. Give him credit not only for a nice looking wife but a nice looking car. He shook my hand, and then took a careful look at all of the drawings hanging on my wall. He started to say something, then noticed the three watercolors on my table. I had not yet put them on the wall.

"What are these?" he asked. "They're really striking."

"Just a study in shades of red, orange, and yellow," I replied. No point in telling him about the flames.

His eyes dilated, I hoped with the pleasure of looking at the watercolors. "There's something more in those images - an intensity, an inner life in the flames, that I've never seen before. I may have a buyer for these. Are you interested?"

I shook my head yes and we discussed terms. I quoted prices in the thousands of dollars, far more than I was accustomed to getting for my work.

He nodded, said he be in touch, and left.

He came back the next day and paid me my price for all three of the watercolors. It started to rain after he left, and heavily, but I barely noticed. I was too busy painting.

***

I sold 10 paintings to him over the next few weeks. He paid cash for all of them.   I paid all of my bills, got up to date in my alimony, and even bought my daughter a birthday present that was close to her heart -- front row tickets to a Thom Yorke concert.

"Is this all the same buyer or a group of people?" I asked the dealer, as he left with the eleventh and twelfth of my efforts.

"I really can't tell you," he replied, softly. "You understand."

I guess I did. Dealers had to keep the buyers out of contact with the painters, otherwise the painters could deal with the buyers directly.

But I needed to know. Who was this wealthy buyer who was saving my life?

I came up with a plan. I began including faint outlines of people in my watercolors of the flames. I put in one face in particular.

And sure enough, there's was a knock of my door one evening, three days after I'd sold the watercolors with the flames and the faces.

Lanterna entered and smiled at me. "I see you haven't taken advantage of the nasty weather we've been having," she said.

"No, otherwise occupied," I replied. "I just knew you were the buyer," I told her, and she sat at the table and regarded a watercolor I had just finished, which had her face.

"A logical deduction," she replied.

"And ... you're not angry that I'm doing this?" I said, "getting word out to the world, or images out to the world, of the flames?"

"Well, as long as I keep buying them, you're only getting word out to me," Lanterna said. "And not the world, not just yet. The flames and what they do are secret."

"Wouldn't it be easier to kill me?" I half joked.

"Certainly cheaper," she replied. "But we're not murderers."

"Good to know," I said.

"And besides," she continued, "your watercolors provide a record of the flames very precious to me and my kind.   The flames evade portrayal by chemical or digital photography. They just look like, well, conventional, unremarkable flames when photographed. Your talent captures something of their true beauty and power."

"Thank you," I said, genuinely touched by her words. "Would you care for some wine, a bite to eat?" I was in a celebratory mood.

"I think I would," Lanterna said and smiled.

I gestured for her to sit at the table.

"How did you know I could walk from here to New York through the flame?" I asked her.

Lanterna smiled. "I saw some of your work in town. I could see that you had a special kind of eye for light ... people with such vision have a high likelihood of being sensitive to the flames, to be able to jaunt home and back or sometimes even farther.

But I have a confession to make -- what I told you about needing to be cleansed was a bit of fib. I wanted to slow you down a bit, give you time to think. And when you started painting them, what wonders you captured. Waiting for the rain was the perfect prescription."

I went to get the wine, and looked at the last illustration I had put on the wall. The last train to Margaretville. It would be the last train to Margaretville or anywhere I'd be drawing for a long time. From now on the only mode of transport I would be painting were those glorious flames.

ABOUT THE AUTHOR

Paul Levinson

Paul Levinson, PhD, is Professor at Fordham University. His science fiction novels include The Silk Code (winner of the Locus Award for Best First Science Fiction Novel of 1999), The Consciousness Plague, The Pixel Eye, Borrowed Tides, The Plot to Save Socrates, Unburning  Alexandria, and Chronica. His novelette "The Chronology Protection Case" was made into a short film and is on Amazon Prime Video. His alternate history story about The Beatles, "It's Real Life," was made into a radio play, and was a finalist for the Sidewise Award for Alternate History. His novelette, "Robinson Calculator," was published in the Robots Through the Ages anthology in July 2023. His nonfiction books, including The Soft Edge, Digital McLuhan, and New New Media, have been translated into 15 languages. He has appeared on CBS, CNN, MSNBC, the History Channel, and NPR. His 1972 album, Twice Upon A Rhyme, was re-issued in Japan and Korea in 2008, and in the U. K. in 2010. His first new album since 1972, Welcome Up: Songs of Space and Time, was released by Old Bear Records and Light in the Attic Records in 2020.

PRAISE FOR AUTHOR

Marilyn and Monet is a wonderful, beautiful story about how art transcends time."

"a truly inspired short story involving the band ... Levinson's It's Real Life is totally original, fascinating and a lot of fun"

BOOKS BY THIS AUTHOR

The Plot To Save Socrates

Book 1 of Sierra Waters trilogy: In the year 2042, Sierra, a young graduate student in Classics, is shown a new dialog of Socrates, recently discovered, in which a time traveler tries to argue that Socrates might escape death by travel to the future! Thomas, the elderly scholar who has shown her the document, disappears, and Sierra immediately begins to track down the provenance of the manuscript with the help of her classical scholar boyfriend, Max.

The trail leads her to time machines in gentlemen's clubs in London and in New York, and into the past--and to a time traveler from the future, posing as Heron of Alexandria in 150 AD. Complications, mysteries, travels, and time loops proliferate as Sierra tries to discern who is planning to save the greatest philosopher in human history. Fascinating historical characters from Alcibiades to William Henry Appleton, the great nineteenth-century American publisher, to Hypatia and Socrates himself appear. With surprises in every chapter.

Unburning Alexandria

Book 2 of Sierra Waters trilogy: Mid-twenty-first century time traveler Sierra Waters, fresh from her mission to save Socrates from the hemlock, is determined to alter history yet again, by saving the ancient Library of Alexandria - where as many as 750,000 one-of-a-kind texts were lost, an event described by many as "one of the greatest intellectual catastrophes in history."

Along the way she will encounter old friends such as William Henry Appleton the great 19th century American publisher and enemies like the enigmatic time travelling inventor Heron of Alexandria. And her quest will involve such other real historic personages as Hypatia, Cleopatra's sister Arsinoe, Ptolemy the astronomer, and St. Augustine - again placing her friends, her loved-ones, and herself in deadly jeopardy.

In this sequel to THE PLOT TO SAVE SOCRATES, award winning author Paul Levinson offers another time-traveling adventure spanning millennia, full of surprising twists and turns, all the while attempting the seemingly impossible: UNBURNING ALEXANDRIA.

Chronica

Book 3 of Sierra Waters trilogy: Sierra and Max arrive in 2062, and find the world has somewhat changed. Joe Biden was President from 2009-2017, and train travel is much more prominent. Was this due to the scrolls that she rescued from the Library of Alexandria? Heron's Chronica, which describes how to build a time travel device and was one of the texts Sierra saved from burning, has not yet been published, and Sierra soon realizes that Heron is doing everything in his lethal power to prevent that from happening. Her attempt to safeguard the Chronica, which she left in William Henry Appleton's keeping, takes her to the end of the 1890s, where she dines, plots, and otherwise interacts with John Jacob Astor IV, Nikola Tesla, Thomas Edison, J. P. Morgan, film pioneers William Dickson and Edwin Porter, and other denizens of The Gilded Age.

The Silk Code

Book 1 of Phil D'Amato trilogy: Phil D'Amato, an NYC forensic detective (also featured in several of Levinson's popular short stories and two subsequent novels), is caught in an ongoing struggle that dates all the way back to the dawn of humanity on Earth--and one of his best friends is a recent casualty. Unless Phil can unravel the genetic puzzle of the Silk Code, he'll soon be just as dead.

Winner Locus Award for Best First Science Fiction novel of 1999.

Rita Ora used The Silk Code in her November 2016 video promo for Tzenenis.

The Consciousness Plague

Book 2 of Phil D'Amato trilogy: Dr. Phil D' Amato returns from The Silk Code, winner of the Locus Award for Best First Science Fiction Novel of 1999, with another blend of biological science fiction and hard-boiled police-procedural mystery.

Memory itself is the suspect in The Consciousness Plague - more particularly, loss of memory, in slivers of time deducted from a growing number of individuals, which plays havoc with everything from the investigation of serial stranglings to candlelight dinners. D'Amato, NYPD forensic detective, investigates a spate of unusual cases and finds evidence of a bacteria-like organism that has lived in our brains since our origin as a species and may be responsible for our very consciousness.

A new antibiotic crosses the blood-brain barrier and inadvertently kills this essential bug. Phil himself falls victim to this memory hole, and must struggle to get the proper authorities to pay attention before everyone loses so much memory that they forget that they forgot in the first place.

The Pixel Eye

Squirrels are spying on us in the park. Mice may have organic bombs set to go off in their brains. Holograms are taking the place of real people. Phil D'Amato investigates a case that pits civil liberties versus national security as he seeks to ward off a major terrorist attack on near-future New York City. (Nominated for the Prometheus Award, 2004.)

Borrowed Tides

August 2016 brought news - real news, in our reality - that an Earth-like planet was discovered circling Proxima Centauri, the third star in the Alpha Centauri system, just over four light years from Earth. This is exactly what happens in Borrowed Tides, first published in hardcover in 2001, re-issued in Kindle this past April. It tells the story of the first starship to the Alpha Centauri system in 2029, employing a new technology which can move it through deep space at almost half the speed of light. But it requires an enormous amount of fuel, and can only carry enough for a one-way trip. A philosopher of science and his childhood friend, an anthropologist with a specialty in Native American culture, have a daringly bizarre plan, and talk the government into putting them in charge of the Light Through starship voyage.

The Loose Ends Saga

eff Harris goes back in time to prevent the explosion of the space shuttle Challenger, but gets pulled into November 1963, and has 23 years to plan his intervention with the Challenger. He discovers that his actions in the past may result in the Soviet Union continuing in the 21st century. He strives with Laura and Karina to prevent this, and also the murder of John Lennon and the September 11 attacks, but the resilience and interconnections of history make it unlikely that they'll be able to stop all of those calamities, and the personal survival of at least one of them may be incompatible with their goals. The Saga contains Loose Ends - the novella nominated for Hugo, Nebula, and Sturgeon Awards - and its sequels Little Differences, Late Lessons, and Last Calls.

Ian's Ions And Eons

Ian's Ions and Eons is the name of a time-travel agency in the Riverdale neighborhood of the Bronx. This anthology contains the three "Ian" novelettes published thus far: "Ian's Ions and Eons" (2011) "Ian, Isaac, and John" (2011) and "Ian, George, and George" (2013). The time travel stories involve Presidential elections, rock music, television and movies. Real historical personages who appear include Al Gore, George W. Bush, William Rehnquist, David Bowie, John Lennon, Dick Cavett, and Orson Welles.

It's Real Life

Book 1 of Double Realities series: It's 1996, and In this alternate history story of the Beatles, disc jockey Pete Fornatale travels downtown to Grand Central Terminal and finds the world of music that he inhabits is very different.

The Other Car

Book 2 of Double Realities series: James Oleson is beginning to see everything in perfect duplicate - two identical models of cars which are the same down to scuff marks and license plate, two old philosophy books with the same torn pages and inscription in old ink, and twin mail men. Is he losing his mind, or experiencing the birth of a new alternate reality via binary fission?

Extra Credit

Book 3 of Double Realities series: Unexplained charges on Jon's credit card are due to something far more profound than identity theft.

The Wallet

Book 4 of Double Realities series: When Professor Klein gets a call that he dropped his wallet in his office, and discovers he still has the wallet in his pocket, he finds that this is the beginning of far more and quite the opposite of an embarrassment of riches.

The P&A

Book 5 of Double Realities series: Sometimes an anti-crash feature in a new car can work much better than expected.

The Chronology Protection Case

When NYPD forensic detective Phil D'Amato takes a call from a lady physicist about her missing husband, he has no idea that her life, his life, and every other scientist working on a top-secret time travel project will soon be in dire jeopardy. As the number of dead begins to mount, D'Amato starts to realize that the suspect is not any one person or group but something much more sinister and dangerous.

"The Chronology Protection Case" was a finalist for the Nebula Award for Best Science Fiction Novelette of 1995. The story was adapted into a low-budget movie by Jay Kensinger, and an Edgar-nominated radio play by Mark Shanahan.

Marilyn And Monet

It all started in the hot summer of 1960, when Marilyn Monroe walked off the set of The Misfits and began to hear a haunting song in her head, "Goodbye Norma Jean" ...

Robinson Calculator

The Calculators -- a secretive group of androids -- have been living off the radar for centuries or longer. Why are they now burying their dead in plain view?

The Orchard

Book 1 of Exo-Genetic Engineers series: In the 22nd century, humans have discovered numerous planets teeming with life, but none with human-level intelligence. Teams of exo-biologists have been dispatched to the most promising places. The fifth planet of the Beta Hydri system has patches of trees that bear delicious fruit. Will it kill the exo-biologists before they can prove the planet has deliberately planted orchards - a sure sign of intelligent life - and get the news back to Earth?

The Orchard was a finalist for the 1998 Sturgeon Award for Best Short Science Fiction.

The Suspended Fourth

Book 2 of Exo-Genetic Engineers series: Have birds on the second planet of Delta Pavonis been bred to sing songs that warn the inhabitants of deadly danger?

Paul Levinson Talks To Rufus Sewell About The Man In The High Castle

Transcript of Paul Levinson's 90-minute interview with Rufus Sewell about The Man in the High Castle television series, along with Paul Levinson's reviews of the series written shortly after the episodes streamed on Prime Video.

www.ingramcontent.com/pod-product-compliance
Lightning Source LLC
Chambersburg PA
CBHW071956230626
47052CB00014B/1195